I0624608

CONTENTS

ACKNOWLEDGMENTS

I gratefully acknowledge Charles Dickens, the author of the famous, "A Christmas Carol". I was inspired by his ideas and used them for my own purposes. I respectfully defer to him for the originality, genius and timelessness of his insightful work.

An American Christmas Carol

or

The Reformation of a Senator

S.M. Conklin Copyright © 2013 S.M. Conklin

ISBN: 0615933629
ISBN-13:978-0615933627 (Publius2)

DEDICATION

This book is dedicated to little people everywhere.

CHAPTER 1
A SHORT INTERVIEW WITH THE OLD GENTLEMAN

The limo rolled through the streets of downtown, sleek and black, its windows beaded with the melting sleet, the noise of pedestrians, beggars and the blaring horns of the cabbies going unheard of behind the glass. The Senate majority leader leant back and poured himself a whiskey,

'Why don't you take the edge off nephew? I find it helps a man to relax at the end of a tough day.'

'No, thank you Uncle, I want to talk seriously to you while I have the chance, are you sure you cannot come to the meeting tonight?'

The elder man looked away from the earnest gaze of his sister's only child. He wished there was something he had on him, some blemish, he was too happy, too secure, it made him uncomfortable. He downed the drink and poured himself another,

'I am far too busy with this upcoming battle, besides, what would I want to hear from a lot of angry tea baggers? There is nothing I can do at this point, the legislation has passed, and there is nothing they can do to stop it and I don't want to stop it. Look, there's a bunch of them now', he nodded his head toward the front of one of the buildings they were slowing down to pass, the people careening around, and hundreds of protestors lined up, obviously freezing in the cold, holding up their signs, Life, Liberty and the Pursuit of Happiness,

'Fools, what do they think they are going to accomplish? The media will have made mincemeat of them by tomorrow.' He looked back at his nephew. The younger man was looking at him intently,

'Uncle, I love you, but this legislation is the last straw, consider how many people it has hurt already, how could you do it knowing that alone?'

'Nonsense, you don't make an omelet without breaking a few eggs, this is for the good of everyone, we have to do this, we have no choice. Its too late anyway.'

'Uncle, please come to the meeting and listen to us, we would love to have you, I hope you reconsider.' He tapped on the glass as he spoke, and the driver opened the communicating window,

'Let me off here Charlie',

'Ok sir'. He leaned forward and grasped the handle of the door to let himself out.

'Uncle, the entire premise of this bill is wrong, but you can change it to focus on creating an environment for the most competition possible, to make the government's role about increasing competition, instead of handing out favors after they take their share? How about having it be about what is best for the little people for once?' He got out and shut the door before his Uncle could respond, gave him an earnest smile and mouthed, "Think about it" and waved as he headed back toward the protestors.

'Bah, just the type of airheaded nonsense these people are spewing out, idealistic fools, it's enough to put me in a foul mood.' He muttered to himself and fed on his inner demons as his driver headed toward his nearby mansion. This city was not what it was when he first came here 35 years ago. Beggars frequently roamed the downtown shelled out areas, while the suburban neighborhoods became increasingly gated to keep the urban pressure out . He would have to speak to his driver about taking a different route home. While the city was still beautiful, he did not like the furtive, desperate looks he was seeing in the eyes of the people walking the streets or waiting for the metrobus as he went by. He didn't feel safe. He leant back into the leather seats, as the gates opened to his driveway. James was still there, he could see the lights on in the kitchen. His mansion was a spectacular example of Georgian architecture. He spent a fortune on the landscaping alone to set off the brick and mortar to perfection. A single man his entire life, he knew how to live well, his entryway was marble with a uniquely designed spiral staircase to the second floor, chandeliers to set off the original paintings and sculptures. James walked in.

'I thought I heard you, would you like some Lafitte in the library?'

'Perfect thank you.'

'I made a roast for dinner, I will take it out now and then I am off.'

'Have a good night James, and thank you.'

'Is there anything you need before you go?'

'Unfortunately, yes and I am sorry to have to tell you this, but, my nephew stopped by and invited himself for Christmas dinner. Can you get the guest suite ready tomorrow? He and his infernal family are going to be here for a few days. Giant pains in my arse. You know it upsets my routine when they push themselves on me. Damn Christmas holiday, why can't they take themselves elsewhere?'

'Very good Sir, consider it done.' He turned and shut the library door softly. The Senator reached under his desk, pushed a switch and the lights came on and his favorite opera started playing He sighed in comfort as he opened the bottle James had brought in and sat down to study the two new paintings he had just purchased that he had had mounted on the opposite wall. The library was deep mahogany, the lighting perfect, the leather chair made according to his design. He felt far away from the city and its rough, dirty, working crowd.

CHAPTER 2
LEST OLD ACQUAINTANCE BE FORGOT

The Senator stepped out of the steamy shower and stepped into his bathrobe. That was an incredible dinner, he would have to commend James. He particularly enjoyed relaxing with good food and wine when he was dining alone. If he felt like company, he knew how to get it, but as he had gotten older and grayer, a small delicious meal and a good port afterward was worth its' weight in gold. He can't remember when he started preferring it to the tattle of voices at a dinner party or a fancy restaurant, a furred beauty by his side, he had no trouble getting female companionship, but he got bored or restless after a couple of months and no one could "get their hooks" into him. At one time he was on the lists of most eligible bachelors, but that time was long past.

He had just dimmed his lights when he heard something. There it was again. It was some kind of slow clanking noise. Had James forgotten a window? On a night like this? He got out of bed and went to the window, the sleet was blowing hard against the panes. It must be that a sash had gotten open. Wait. It was getting louder. He stood as if turned to stone when he heard his name being called. 'Ronald Greenlaw'. The voice sounded familiar. He shook himself. What was going on? Was it the wine? Was he hallucinating? He listened again breathless, his heart beating faster against his chest. There was nothing. He let out a sigh and started to walk back toward his bed when he could not believe his eyes. His door handle was slowly turning, he heard the clanking and something came into the room. In the dim light and soft dark oriental carpet the specter glided across the room, dragging chains with heavy links with him as the Senator stood stock still in stunned silence until it was almost upon him. He shrank away in horror, this specter was vaguely familiar.

'What do you want? Who are you? Is this some kind of joke?'

'Ronald Greenlaw, don't you recognize me? In life I was your mentor when you entered the Senate. You replaced me as Majority leader when I passed out of earthly life.' The specter was just that, his voice unearthly and eerie with a long moaning quality that made his hair stand on end.

'What? Mr. Burke, I must be dreaming. No. No.' He rubbed his eyes and felt the roast turning in his stomach.

'You are not dreaming.' The specter's ghostly eyes bore down on the Senator as he cowered and felt his knees shake, he felt a chair behind him and gratefully sank gingerly on its edge, almost afraid that it would not be real. His mind could not grasp what he was experiencing.

'What are you doing here? What do you want with me? Why are you in chains? You were always about the people's business. For god's sake go back to where you came from and leave me in peace!'

'Peace? Is it Peace you want?' The specter shook his chains violently and his ghostly voice rose to a shriek as he vented his anger.

'I am here for that very reason. The peace you currently enjoy will not be yours when you leave this earth. I am here to bear witness to you what will happen, if you continue on your current course, as I and many others have done before you.' The specter came closer and yet closer and touched his arm with his ghostly sleeve. Instantly there was a whirlwind of activity, it was as if he was Dorothy in the wizard of Oz, the bed was swirling, the clothes were churning, lamps and desks were going around and around them as they pushed up through the center of everything and then out above it all to some other beyond. Ghostly faces and similar specters appeared and disappeared, some with chains which looked as if they were dragging them so heavily they could not move and yet they did. He looked this way and that, he recognized the faces! The tyrants of old…there was King George III, there was Catherine the Great, The Sun King, and the later period tyrants, Lenin, Hitler, Stalin, Mussolini, then countless faceless politicians, there was Roosevelt and Johnson, he was sure that was Lyndon B. Johnson he just saw. He could not draw his eyes away from Johnson's plight. Heavy burdens weighed him, a frightful, dreadful agony was etched permanently into his distorted features, what could he have done to deserve this? His mind was whirling he could not believe and yet there they were before his eyes. They were suspended and they all had the same haunting deathly agonizing stare. They were carrying painful burdens and their visages alike conveyed infinite suffering. In an instant he had absorbed it all and in an instant the specter released him to his bedroom. He had gotten a glimpse.

'No, it cannot be true, this cannot be, this is something out of a movie, some fiction or other', his mind repeated as he looked up incredulous and trembled on the edge of the chair. Yet somewhere in the back of his mind he recognized a growing fear as he had advanced in his years. He had been afraid of the very thing the specter had revealed.

'This will be your lot. Remember what you have seen.'

'But what does it mean? What am I to do?' The specter seemed to be slipping away.

'I must go, I cannot stay, I am doomed but there is still time for you. Remember what you have seen.'

'No. Don't leave me. Explain this!'

The specter was now at the door, dragging his heavy chains, he turned and his empty eye sockets looked into the Senators once more.

'You will be visited this night by three spirits. There is still time for you. The first will come at the stroke of one. Attend them and learn what will redeem you: Repeal, Repeal, Repeal!!!' His voice rising to a shriek, he slipped out the door, his chains echoing down the staircase until all at once, there was nothing. No sound except the sleet against the window pane. The senator moved with a start, slipped off the chair and fell heavily. Stunned, he shakily recovered himself and turned the lights on. His room was empty, no sound of clanking chains, no spinning lamps and beds. Had he dreamed this? Did he just pass out?

'Bahh, it must have been a bit of bad meat. What a trick. That was all. Hahahahah.' He was still shaking and looked down at his hand in the light. He might have to change his mind about female companionship, what the hell kind of a dream was that?

'Hahahahahahahahah' He laughed loudly and long and was still chuckling to himself as he turned out his light. He shook his head, grabbed a swig of the whiskey that was at his bedside table and slipped quickly and deeply into unconscious sleep.

CHAPTER 3
PAST ENDEAVORS

The light was blazing in his room.

'What the devil?' He jerked awake and blinked in the bright light coming from the entrance to his room.

'Who are you?'

'I am the spirit who it was foretold to you would come.'

'I can't see you what is wrong with the lights, they are too bright.' As he said this, he saw a blazing figure standing tall, gown flowing, it looked like…the Statue of Liberty.

'Lady Liberty, this is too much, turn down the light, please.' He could not help but see humor in this dream, for that is what it must be. He decided he would go along, he knew he would wake up.

'Ronald, we are going on a short journey, prepare yourself.' She came closer, and now the light was so bright that he could see nothing but light. When the lights faded, he could see an office, he recognized it, it was in Baltimore, he knew this place.

'Who is that? Why it is Judge Thornton! I have not seen him in years. Judge, Judge, how have you been?' He tried to reach out and touch him but the Judge ignored him, walked right by him and, leaning over the back of a young man's chair he perused what the younger man was writing.

'Remember Ronnie, that laws that are simple and just are the greatest benefactors of mankind.'

It was then that he saw the younger man's face. It was him as a young man! It all came back, he remembered the office, the intense work they did as interns for the judge. They worked hard and loved it. His friend Sam was there right next to him.

'Sam Woodward. God he was a good soul.' His friend Sam was an inspiration to him and he remembered their good natured competition and camaraderie. The late nights and the pub visits after an opinion was written that was critical to restoring justice. How Judge Thornton had congratulated them on a job well done. It all came rushing back. Sam had come from the inner city and escaped poverty by working hard at getting the best grades in his school. He had known what he wanted to do when he was very young and when he got into Georgetown, tears had run down his mother's face when he read the acceptance letter to her. Sam. What great work we did back then. A flood of emotions filled his heart, he remembered how good it felt. Having a beer with his friend and debating long after work was done, he had forgotten those feelings, feelings that their job really meant something. It was a pure emotion, a gut feeling back then. He had not felt that in years. He wanted to look away but could not tear his eyes away from the scene. The Judge continued.

'Ronnie, our constitution is the most important document in the history of mankind for helping the little people. The purpose of it is to ensure that our laws are just. Also that they apply equally to all. This is the most important function. Just laws limit the size and scope of government's power and thus free the people from fearing the law. Man's history has never protected the little people in this way, and judges in this country have a critical job in ensuring the constitution is abided by. It is how you preserve the foundations for future generations to build on.' Judge Thornton was a wise man, advanced in years at the time Ronnie was a young man.

'But laws are made to help the people. The people want the laws to do this.' He remembered his stubborn refusal to believe that governments should not use their power for what the people wanted.

'Ronnie, the public good cannot be advanced through the expansion of governmental administrative authority, tell me why.' The younger Ronnie sighed.

'Because it must necessarily take property for its own existence.' He said it with resignation and the elder man smiled.

'Correct. Take it to a logical conclusion.' The younger man thought for a few minutes and responded.

'If it could be used to "help" the public in one area, it will soon expand to all areas of a society, and by necessity it will become an immense material burden to the very society it is purporting to help.'

'And thereby, it takes the life of the people it is supposed to be helping, because they use their life to pursue their happiness, in effect, create their livelihoods. Thus, expansive government enslaves and you know that is not gonna fly with me.' This was from Sam, who could never resist interjecting in any discussion of the constitution.

'Ronnie, I believe you will come to understand the beauty of our constitution when it is interpreted strictly. When our laws abide by it, the people are free to pursue their happiness in peace. That is the very definition of public good for all time. They can go about the wonderful business of their lives free of the worry of an overbearing governmental authority bent on tyranny.'

'And they love the law because it is applied equally to all.' This was Sam again, his wide smile revealing a perfect set of bright teeth in his dark face. It was a trademark smile and made everyone who met him love him instantly.

'It is a life's work defending the little people, defending limits on government, it seems inevitable that governments expand. It takes a tough, clear mind in the judge's seat to set the correct course for the law.' The old man had made it his life's work. The creases and good nature that defined his face were a testament to a job he loved, for it was centered in the belief in his neighbor, and a belief that God had created a perfect world, with liberty (to choose good or evil) and justice (the natural consequence of the choice) for all. Just laws in society are in harmony with what God created and good and evil are not relative terms.

'Now boys, it is time to close up shop, we will prepare the brief on Monday, we need to get to the King's Lion in time for the Christmas party!. Shut down those screens and hurry up!' The lighthearted gaiety was sublime, the happy character of the Judge was a wonderful thing to be near.

The old Senator turned to Lady Liberty, the bittersweet pain he was feeling evident on his face.

'A great man. We truly loved working for him. He died too soon.' She looked at him,

'You revered this man? Did you take his wisdom to heart and carry it, expand on it and take it with you throughout life? This would be a great gift to someone you loved.'

Before he could answer, the vision before him vanished and he found they were at the King Lion's Pub, their favorite local watering hole, and the scene was the festivities of a Christmas party. All were dressed smartly and respectfully, happy smiles on the members of law firms and their families. Understanding each other and happy to celebrate a year's end to good work the link between them could be felt by anyone entering the room. He saw himself there, a good looking young man, in his twenties, several young women were trying to talk to him but he was standing his back to the bar, looking for someone or something.

'Oh no. Please, can we go back?' Lady Liberty looked at the scene.

'You seem happy here, you are looking for someone?' He saw a smile light up his young face and he felt a wrenching in his breast. Painful feelings that he strove for many years to subdue returned with an incredible rushing force. A girl walked into the pub with several friends, talking and laughing, saw him and a smile lit up her eyes, she was obviously delighted to see him. She was lively and high spirited, she lit up the room with her presence and several people looked at them when she rushed over to him and greeted him with a kiss. She was a slip of a thing for all that she was full of life, and the young man grabbed her around her waist and twirled her around looking as if he would never set her down again.

'I thought I would never get out of court.' She was breathless, her eyes dancing, she obviously had something fun to tell.

'Tough fight?'

'Awful. We are still in the the middle of it but the Judge gave us a reprieve and we all got to go home. I think both sides gave a shout when she announced it, much to her chagrin.' The young man laughed. She was smiling and happy, they were looking forward to a fun evening.

'I can imagine the scene. She hates disruption in "her court", remember when that kid dropped a video game in the court and it started bleeping and making noise, I thought her head would explode!'

'I know it, the whole court burst out laughing just looking at her face.' The two collapsed themselves into laughter and of the two ghost visitors looking down at the scene only the Senator looked pained.

'Please, please Lady..' he trailed off. She stood firmly rooted to the spot observing the party.

'You look very happy. What happened to her?' Instantly a light flashed and they were transported to a graveyard. The rain was pouring down and hundreds of people were lined up around a grave.

'Here lies Judge Thornton, a beloved and impartial judge, who will now be judged,' read the tombstone. He saw himself there, remembered how the grief had stricken them all, saw Beatrice, the Judge's daughter crying by the casket as he held on to her hand. The lovely, lively girl from the Christmas party was engulfed in tears, bravely holding it together. When the final visitors left, just she and he stood by the grave. She turned to him and finally spoke,

Thank you for everything Ronnie, you know I love you so much. I hate to do this, but I have to say Goodbye. I have thought it over clearly and I cannot go with you.'

'Why? Beatrice, we are going to get married, what are you talking about?'

'I cannot. I cannot marry you.' She looked

incredibly sad, even sadder than the graveyard and gravesite, and gray day and rain.

'Beatrice, I do not understand.'

'You have found something that will never be able to satisfy, you are going down a path that I cannot follow you on.'

'Beatrice, you are wrong, this will be good for us, we can finally get somewhere. Go to DC where it all happens. Be a part of the group that changes this country. What do you mean you cannot follow me?'

'You have fallen in love with power, and now it is taken hold of you and I cannot stand next to you and be supportive. I have watched you in this campaign, you have made promises, you have lied, said things I would never have believed of you. Not the old you. But you have changed. Since you stopped working for father and started running for election, you are different. It happened slowly, first a little lie here and there, a small promise, then you were elected, and now, it is almost as if you are unmoored. Nothing is too small to promise, or, too big.'

'Beatrice. That is only a game, it is the game of politics, it can't touch us, it can't hurt us, it cannot change the fact that I love you. I am going to do good work in Washington, with you by my side how could I fail. Seriously, look at me, you cannot leave now.' She looked at him steadily.

'No. It can hurt us and it will. I know it as surely as I am standing here, that these promises are empty and at best will hurt you and at worst will hurt many. No.'

'Beatrice, don't do this to us, don't do this to me.'

'No Ronnie. Know that I love you with all my heart, but I cannot go to DC and watch you do this.'

The old Senator looking at this scene felt his cheeks wet and became angry,

'You stupid fool, why did you ever let her walk away? You fool!' He yelled at the motionless figure standing alone at the graveyard. The girl had turned and walked away under her umbrella, and the young man stood there in the rain turning the ring over and over in his fingers.

'Go after her, you stupid ass. Oh damn it Lady, please release me'. He covered his face with his hands hopelessly trying to remove the scenes from his consciousness, overcome with emotion he spoke softly, 'Please. No more.'

His bedroom looked and felt empty as he looked around, all the scenes vanishing before his eyes. Lady Liberty had plumbed depths that he had thought had long ago vanished, but they were still there and he was forced to reckon with them. He felt immensely burdened and tired.

'Curse this night.'

He looked at the clock, it was nearly 2 am. He felt a dread as he watched the minute hand of the clock tick toward the top of the hour.

CHAPTER 4
PRESENT HAPPENINGS

The two visitors stood outside one of the windows and looked in. The big man with his big voice boomed in his ear,

'Let's take a look at what is happening in here, this looks like a prospering existence.' The second spirit had arrived on time, announcing to him that he had no time to waste, he needed to enlighten him on the current state of things.

'What things? I am not going anywhere.' The old Senator had asked, he was in a surly mood after Lady Liberty's visit and did not like these dreams he was having, they felt like nightmares. The big man would not elaborate and touched his sleeve.

They were in a busy suburb of Alexandria, a wealthy neighborhood outside of DC where the money flowed from Senators and Congressmen to lobbyists and aids and organizations and all the deputies, ministers, aides, and bureaucrats that were the necessary result of endless government expansion. Created from Executive Order these departments filled with bureaucrats were all tasked with missions of "public good". While they were doing the good, they lived in well made expensive houses, sent their children to the best schools, had mandatory salary increases, drove fancy cars, had all the latest in technology at their disposal, their offices were air conditioned in the summer and heated in the winter. Dental plans, pension plans, 401K plans, plenty of paid vacation time and paid sick days there was never enough money for their departments, there was never enough money for them to do the public good, and they were always in the right because they wanted more "public good". The public good was filled with special interests they were in charge of doling out someone else's money to, of course they wanted more public good. That's what kept them in clover.

The two men looked through the window, one of them immense in height and breadth, powerful, present, the other slightly hunched, gray, older than his years. They could see the furnishings inside were tasteful, it was obvious that the family that lived there were not used to hardship in any way. Groceries were piled high in the kitchen, the television was playing one of the mainstream nightly news programs and two children were sitting on the couch playing on their computers. The mom was drinking wine and talking on the phone and the dad was having a beer in the library, just beyond her, from their view, looking into a computer screen himself.

'Honey, that was Bridget. She says that Martha is calling a meeting for the Union reps. You are going to have to get everyone together.'

'I already know. We are down to the final negotiations. It is already a done deal, we are going to get everything we want. They don't have a leg to stand on.'

'Yes, but you have to meet, she says they are working on some last minute strategies.'

'What is she worried about? We have them by the nuts. We get our raises plus 100 percent medical or we shut down the government, and you know how that always makes them crumble.'

'I think there is more too it this time. I think they want more control. They have some more people they want taken care, some other groups this time, I think they are very powerful too. Could mean we won't have to worry about our jobs for a good long time…I think you better listen to her. You will have to get everyone together-Christmas is a great time to make it all happen.'

'They should be happy with the increases they are getting and I know for a fact that we are going to make sure we get everything. That shutdown did the trick. It made the other party a four letter word Ha! Remember that?'

'I know, I loved how Myrna and Joe on the morning show took that and ran with it two years ago. Boy did they make those tea baggers look like a bunch of mean rednecks that don't want education, clean energy or to help to the poor. It was fantastic!' Her husband laughed.

'The next day we all gave fifths of Stoli to Joe at the club and high fived him.'

The big man by his side turned to him,

'These people do the "public good" by your orders? What exactly kind of good is it that they are extorting for? Is blackmail their job? What department is it that they work for? Who are these groups they are blackmailing you for?' The old man knew the answer and mumbled something about them being part of the Department of Education, the wife anyway. He recognized her and he thought he recognized the husband as being in the Environmental Protection Agency. They were both higher ups, he knew that at least. He shrugged,

'So what? They have to fight for what they have just like everyone else. Why shouldn't they get what they want, they are part of the society too.' He said it, but it sounded hollow, even to him. The big man reminded him of someone, someone recent, a big man with a bigger voice, full of life, full of the present, when in his presence you felt as if he understood you, your bad parts and good, the entirety of you because…maybe… he was you. A larger more engaged, larger than life you, aware of the present state of being. The big man's eyes looked deeply into his. Suddenly he understood, he saw it all in a flash of overwhelming understanding. The oxygen hit his brain like cocaine as he took a deep breath. The Great Society. The Departments were the result of The Great Society. That is what Johnson had done. The Congress, his Congress, his House of Representatives and Senate, was no longer the august and venerated body of and for the people that it had been. It was now a manager of administrators of The Great Society, dealing with only who gets what and how much. Worse than that, Congress was being extorted by the very bodies that it was managing. The Senate, him, himself, his job was no longer the highest office in the land, it was a job that any lacky running a bunch of franchised gas stations could easily do. That is why Johnson did it. He resented the power we had. The old Senator let out his held in breath. The Congress had become a bunch of micro-managing administrators managing other administrators. The two houses were no longer deliberating on matters of public policy, on matters that were essential to the republic, it was no longer deliberating, full stop. The entire body were pawns. He shook his head as if shaking his head would make it not true.

'How did this happen? How did the Senate sink this low? How is it possible that we lost our power? We have constitutional authority to decide important matters for the country. How did we lose that power?'

'Dude…the law has to abide. What happens when the law does not abide?' The big man opened up his coat and a Pandora's box of knowledge started pouring out. The first bit of knowledge hit him.

'Three branches. Executive, Legislative and Judicial. We are one of the big three.'

'Dude..look again.'

'Oh.'

There was a fourth, the one he had just witnessed outside the window. The one he was instrumental in creating, the massive bureaucracy of the administrative state, what has become a chicago like mob arm of the federal government.

'You ask how? Come on. You know how.' At this, the old Senator stuck out his chin in derisive defiance.

'We had to do what we did to get elected so we could do the people's business. Yea, when we make promises elections go the right way. So we take care of our special interests. Its politics. I do what I have to do.' The big man raised his eyebrows and looked over his sunglasses at him, then pushed them back up when the old Senator could not hold his gaze and looked away.

'You know there is no administrative function for the federal government within a constitutional framework, LBJ went around it and Congress agreed. You guys gave up your power! You wanted to use it to get elected and poooffff the executive budget was approved by Congress.'

'But that was before my time!' The Senate Majority leader said loudly and sullenly. The big man opened up his coat and he was overwhelmed with the size of the many departments he saw.

'True. But look what "politics" has done. The present day is the result of this small misstep.'

'The public wanted all this. Plus, we gave the agencies specific directives and mission statements. They were supposed to be carrying these out. A trillion dollars can't be wrong.'

'Yesssssss, the agencies help…. they help themselves to more. And what are you in this whole scheme? I thought you were the ones supposed to be writing law. Doesn't look like it now. You have a ton of agencies writing laws for you. Dude. Your job is obsolete.' The big man closed his coat and looked down at him. The Great Society. The old Senator thought of the myriad of agencies, the endless departments. Trillions of dollars could not be wrong. They just couldn't be. In spite of this meager comfort, he could take no comfort in the solid realization that his job, once the most venerated position in the land, did not require anything more than a McDonald's or Starbuck's manager training program.

'No.' His mind would not accept it, he resented this big man with his big coat and his rational look at what is. His thoughts started running away as they walked away from the house. 'This is not what the Senate is today. I am the leader. We just voted on…oh jesus…the health care law. Good lord,' he muttered. He realized they had not deliberated on anything other than how to pay for it. It was 2,500 pages of new authority for the Health and Human Services Department to write rules and regulations for every doctor or hospital taking care of every single human being that was born in this country. He had not even read it. 'Why didn't I see this before? Damn it. I will not be the one presiding over this. I will not be a low life manager of a bunch of stinking bureaucrats, I will not...' He had no time for any more soliloquy, the big man had touched his sleeve and they were no longer in Alexandria.

The farmer looked over the fields and pointed to the right.

'We could not get on the lower lots, too much rain this spring so we seeded the rye on number 68. Here it is, it looks fantastic doesn't it? We were able to bale it before it went to seed and now I have some high quality clean straw. I can plow it down in the spring and plant sweet corn here and tomatoes over there.' The farmer pointed to different parts of the field. They could see the field was green, having recovered from the cutting and grown through the fall, it looked healthy and lush, and was free of weeds.

'Well, unfortunately that field was not on our list, so, we can't compensate anything for that one.' The big man and the old senator were walking with a farmer and what appeared to be a government agent from the USDA.

'Have you thought about joining the land conservation?'

'Joe, we need to access more land to rotate our crops. That would restrict the size of our farm.' They were walking and talking. The USDA rep was holding a clip board.

'What I really need is the lower ditches cleaned, particularly the one that the county has been cleaning for 100 years and now, well, the last twenty years or so it has been silting up.' The farmer was pointing to a lowland area that looked like it was overgrown, good sized trees were in the ditches.

'You could do it Joe, get on the excavator, quit this job and tell them the position no longer exists. You can run the excavator.' The USDA rep looked sheepish.

'Well. That is not my department, I think they require

all sorts of permitting for that kind of dredging. Let's walk up the back 40 and see if we can get you anything for rotation there.' Apparently if the rotation was not done the way it was planned on the clipboard, the money would not get paid.

'Joe, about this contract…we need to get rid of it. A couple of hundred dollars maybe, if all the paperwork is in order, which by the way we are not compensated for the time it takes. You need to remove us from this whole thing, it was a bad idea from the start. I should not have let you guys talk us into it.' The farmer went on to talk seriously with the other man about the burden of taxation that made his business increasingly more difficult to have any money at the end of the day to invest back into it.

'Every stick of lumber, every gallon of fuel, every fan belt and part of a tractor, a large part of the cost we pay for those goes to the government. We are shouldering these costs, while the price of broccoli has remained pretty constant over the last twenty years. My grandfathers could afford to keep the houses that are part of the farm. We are lucky to keep roofs on them. Not to mention the local school taxes. I should have razed those buildings when I had the chance.' They looked at the old buildings, wooden structures that were built long ago but were not what they once were.

'I know, its tough. And don't worry about the contract, the money will just go away.' He was nice, sympathetic. The big man turned to the old senator.

'This is the farm bill isn't it. The great farm bill that must be passed or farms will go under. Really? Wow, farm welfare at work. The USDA reps get an office, a nice car, a pension plan, the farmer gets paperwork and a promise of a few dollars piddled into his hand and the money just disappears…poofff!' The big man moved his hands up, splaying the fingers of his wide hands up in the air as if all the money was there and then vanished.

'Take a close look.' He let his sunglasses slip down his

nose and looked at the old man with a penetrating look. The Senator had no choice when the Pandora's box of that giant coat opened again and the second wave of knowledge came swirling out. He saw the price that was being paid by every small business, bottom line after bottom line came up, businesses and families under incredible stress to keep their livelihoods going.

'Enough! Ok, OK..I get it..' The old Senator looked away. He thought with disgust, 'It just doesn't work. It is too much. The people cannot take much more.'

CHAPTER 5
BACK TO THE FUTURE

He felt cold. The figure next to him was radiating cold. When he had stood next to the big man, he could feel the warmth radiating, this was like standing next to an ice chunk. They were standing on something and looking out. It was something high, he had a sudden fear. The figure next to him handed him a pair of binoculars and he looked through them without saying a word.

When 3 am had come he had been ready. He was sitting with his overcoat on, in his room. After the big man had left he willed himself to stay awake. He would try to prevent this third visit. But precisely at 3 am a dreaded apparition began to materialize next to him. He could barely see it, more like feel an icy presence that made him shiver. He looked up and swallowed. There was nothing there, but there was something there. He thought it touched his sleeve.

Looking out through the binoculars he could see everywhere and everything. A shop window was boarded up, there was trash blowing in the streets, broken windows smashed, cars abandoned. He could see some group of younger people run up to one of the shops that still had a window and smash it. What was going on? What was he supposed to be looking at? He pulled the binoculars away from his eyes and turned,

'What am I supposed to be looking at?' The figure did not speak but raised what appeared to be its arm and pointed. He turned back and put the binoculars up to his eyes again. Looking a little further on he could see two people who looked normal sitting in a pub window, as soon as he trained the binoculars on them he could hear their conversation. They were a couple of Joes having a brew, no one he knew.

'What are you going to do?'
'Listen, I know where we can exchange our gold.'

The other man cracked a short smile,

'Yea, right here, but keep it down. Do you want someone to hear us?, keep it down. Its bad enough we are sitting in the window. I still have a bunch of greenbacks. Can we do anything with those?'

'We can see them coming if we sit here. No. They are worthless. Unfortunately, they got us good. When the dollar crashed it crashed hard. All that printing finally caught up. I hear that a small group is trying start a new currency based on a gold standard. A bunch of private citizens are getting together and they are putting their gold behind it. It is secret though at this point, but you can buy the currency and it is good, its actually worth something. I think we should check it out. I have some oil I would like to sell, I have been bartering, but it would be good if we could get a currency established again.'

'I am so disgusted with the whole damn thing. I can't comprehend this.'

'Try to stay well and keep your family together. Who would have thought it would come to this. Did you hear what happened yesterday?'

'Yea. They strung up two more. I can't believe they did it right in the city park, right along the parkway so everyone could see.'

'It is surreal. Like something you read about but would never think you would see. What do you suppose is going to happen when they run through them all?' They sipped their brews, each silently reflecting.

The Senator frowned. The dollar crashed? Impossible.

He looked down another street. 'Ahh here is someone working,' or no, the man wasn't. He was carrying something in a wheelbarrow, what was it? It looked like...fifty dollar bills? He watched mesmerized as the man wheeled the money into what looked like a grocery store and came out with an empty wheelbarrow and a gallon of milk and a loaf of bread which he quickly stashed under his coat. 'What? No. This can't be.' They had analyst upon analyst advising to raise the debt ceiling, basically the federal government could double their spending, print more money and keep interest rates artificially low and everything would work out. Supposedly they did not have to address the debt. This doesn't make sense. Is this some distant future? He turned to the ghostly vision next to him with a questioning look. The face was not visible, turned away from him and looking out over the city and beyond, to the suburbs and farmland. He trained his binoculars in that direction. Slowly panning around the vista, he saw the same thing. Villages and farms with boarded up windows, roofs caved in, no tractors at work, no people walking, no streetlights working, it did not look like America. In the villages there were some people walking there, but they were hurrying and looking around in fear as they scurried hastily along the street. This was obviously a society that was not in a state of happy productivity. More like a frightened group that had shut down and was going to freeze to death. It was as if the heat had been turned off. Everything was cold, dark and damp. Dark smoky fires were belching black smoke from some of the chimneys but did not look as if they produced any heat. What were they burning? What was that smell? Why were gaunt looking dogs running in packs up the streets? He saw no lights lit, no busses running, no trains or planes, no trucks delivering milk, no automobiles.

'Did people run out of fuel? Is there some kind of fuel shortage? Did they finally exhaust the worlds's supply of oil? What was going on? Spirit, why don't you say something? What year is this? Why does America look like a communist country shelled out after a war?'

His mind was remembering the scenes from today, when he was watching people going to and from work, when he was rolling in his limousine through lit up city streets, through well kept suburbs. He had just visited a prospering farm and walked the fields alongside the farmer with the big man. It was a paradise compared to what he saw before him.

'This doesn't make sense. Is this the future of America?' As he asked the question he realized the answer. The world did not run out of oil. This was a result of letting the fourth branch become too powerful. The tyranny of a federal leviathan of bureaucracies and special interest groups that squelch everything as they finally reach their goal of interfering in every private sector pursuit.

'Ronnie, take it to its logical conclusion.' He could hear the Judge's voice echo in his brain. Every form of productivity grinds to a halt when it reaches its goal of mandating control over every pursuit.

'Life, Liberty and the Pursuit...doesn't look like anyone is pursuing anything.'

His questions went unheeded by the cold form standing next to him as he trained the binoculars back on the city that he stood overlooking. Something was coming toward them. A large, noisy group, were moving steadily up the street. 'Ahhhh. Here we go. Maybe I can find something out.' But as they got closer the group had the appearance of an angry mob, they were closely packed, moving like a swarm of killer bees, they had a hold of something and were moving it up the street en masse. He could not make out what it was, but something about their faces told him they were up to no good. He felt a cold dreaded fear well up in side of him. They swarmed around below him and he tried to make out what they were carrying but he could not quite see it. He recognized some faces though. They looked like faces from history, or from his paintings…wasn't that Danton? Or was it the head of the Department of Health and Human Services? And over there, wasn't that Robespierre? Or was it the head of Homeland Security?

'String'm up! String'm up! String'm up!'

'It's New Years Day! Its time for a New Year!'

'We need change. Its time for change. String'm up!'

They were chanting and yelling, fists in the air in anger that would not abate and their voices reached a crescendo as they raised their package above their heads.

The old senator could not quite see what they had, he took the binoculars away from his eyes and looked down, downward just below him.

'What the devil? What am I standing on?' He looked to his left where the ghost had now turned his full face on him, and it conveyed a blackness, and icy doom. He looked down again; he was standing on… 'Ohhhhh' He was standing atop a gallows. He stood in a daze of dawning understanding. That's why they were so high. He started to feel dizzy and looked down at his feet. There was a rope strung around it and just beyond his feet, they had strung someone on the rope, he could see the hat less head, but could not make out the face. The crowd screamed in anger as they pulled on the rope and the body swung by its neck, its' feet straightening out, its hands grabbing its neck, jerking backward and forward. He felt himself begin to sway, no, he was going to fall into their midst. The body swung toward him, he was falling, he finally saw the face…..
'AAAAHHHHHHHH….'

CHAPTER 6
THE AWAKENING

His face was crushed into his bed and he had his pillow in a death grip when James knocked and came into the room.

'Good morning sir, I have brought you some coffee, would you like your breakfast here, or will you be eating downstairs?' The Senate Majority Leader opened one eye. Was he alive? He was not dead? He was not hanging by a noose? He closed his eye and let out a long sigh of relief, he breathed deeply, relished the feeling of his body against the bed sheets, the feeling of his hands at the end of his arms, the feeling of his brain awakening to life. He just lay there in the delicious feeling of being alive.

'Then it did not happen yet. It did not happen yet.'

'What's that sir?'

'James. Is that you? I am so glad to see you. Please, Please, don't bother with any of that. I am getting up directly.'

'James. What year is it?'

'It is still 2013. December 25th 2013.'

'James. You have made me the happiest, happiest of men. Call my nephew at once, at once do you hear? And get a hold of the press secretary, I need to schedule a press conference immediately. No, scratch that, I need to meet with my nephew first, first do you hear?'

'Sir, I hear you, are you ok, you look flushed, can I get you something?, shall I send for the doctor?' The Senator laughed out loud.

'No, No, I am fine. I have too much to do. Get going now, get going.'

'Very good sir.' He jumped out of bed and started pulling clothes out of his closets then stopped. He stood still in thought. He would need to look good. He would need to look his best. He spent the next hour attending to his attire.

The day had been full to the brim and he had never felt

more alive. Everyone had commented on how young he looked, he felt as if he were peeling back the years. He was filled with purpose. 'The people's purpose. While on this earth the good of mankind will be my business.' he could not stop smiling. 'God I have been such a fool, such a stubborn fool.' He prayed a silent pray of thankfulness and a request for guidance.

The day started with breakfast with his nephew, who was overjoyed with this sudden turn of events.

'Uncle. I cannot believe it. I am amazed. You are going to help us. You are going to change everything. You cannot believe what this will mean to everyone. You are going to be a superhero, I can feel it!'

'Nephew, please, this is going to be a difficult fight, we are going to be working on reversing almost 100 years of policy. It is not going to be easy. There is going to be a very large pushback from the special interests. We must get ready.'

'I know that Uncle, but with you, your power of persuasion, you can do so much. People really listen to you and do what you think is right. You are an incredible presence.' The older man looked abashed. The sincere affection and respect he heard in his nephew's voice moved him. He never knew his nephew felt that way about him. He turned away so the younger man could not see how much he was affected.

'Well, we shall see, I do think I can count on a few to be persuaded and they are key players.' He continued. 'There are two things that are paramount, the rest we can tackle later, but we must get started on two immediately. The first is repealing that nasty piece of legislation, the Affordable Health Care Act. The second,' and here he paused, 'is to get started on organizing the states for a constitutional convention.'

'Amen to repealing the health care law, it has been the nail in the coffin for the health care industry but, Uncle, what are you talking about? A constitutional convention?

They won't go for that. They don't want a new constitution, I know these people.'

'Nephew, that is not what I am talking about. Our founding fathers were men that were extremely distrustful of concentrated power. We as a country have been lulled into a false sense of security. We have not paid proper attention to that distrust which has real merit. It is time to give that distrust its' due. They would not agree to the constitution without some safeguards. We need to draw on those safeguards now.'

'I know about the Bill of Rights, Uncle'

'Did you always interrupt in this way? I am speaking of Article the Fifth of the constitution. A convention may be called by the legislatures of two thirds of the states and amendments proposed. The amendments can thus be ratified by three fourths of the states and the constitution thus amended.'

'Uncle, this is brilliant. I think we can do it!'

'It was not my idea, but it is long past time when we should have begun to call for this convention. Congress has given its authority away, and will not be allowed to reform itself. Not by the current mob that is controlling it.' He shuddered for a moment as if a cold hand had swept over him, then shook it off and put his thoughts back into the present.

'We must act to get Congress' authority back, to restore three separate branches of government and take away the fourth branch's power before it is too late. I just hope it is not too late already. Congress alone has the power to deliberate issues for its representatives and it alone has the power to write law and that power will not be usurped by a bunch of bureaucrats who couldn't get a job stocking shelves in a grocery store. Not while I am representing the people and the leader of this august and venerated body. I will make it the rest of my life's work to restore the rightful power to Congress and refocus its mission to keep government authority within proper limits.'

'Uncle. I think you made your first speech of the New Year!' They both laughed and raised two champagne glasses in a toast.

'To you Uncle, may the force be with you.'

'God help us and help me with this upcoming press conference and meeting.' To his nephew he said, 'I expect you here with your family for dinner at 6 o'clock. Do not be late, I want the whole family here, we need to talk about how we are going to save the future.'

'God Bless you Uncle, we will be here in good time.'

'Very well, then, lets get to work!'

The Old Senate Majority Leader had become young again. He went on to have the best speech of his life in a rousing of oratorical fireworks as he called on the members of both houses to regain what they had lost. The speech was clear headed, and full of purpose, it was inspiring and held listeners breathless as their hearts began to soar on the wings that true freedom promises. They knew they were experiencing a great moment in the history of the country, a speech that would be remembered for generations. The news channels played it on Christmas Day and they could not keep up with the demand, a young Senator from Texas posted it on the internet and it went viral. It was the beginning of a new day for the Senate Majority Leader and a new path for the country. He crowned the speech with the words he had been meaning to say since he had woken up this morning, they burst from his chest with a smile on his lips and they echoed through the chambers and for future generations as he called on the members for their first task.. "Repeal! Repeal! Repeal!".

The End

ABOUT THE AUTHOR

Sue Conklin is an American farmer. Like Hector St. John De Crevecoeur during the enlightenment period, who wrote "Letters from an American Farmer" and settled the farm where she was born, she loves America. She loves history, biography, her family, learning and farming. She spends her time between her family farm (Pine Hill Farm) in Orange County, NY and with her husband and family in Westford, VT. During the winter months when not farming she enjoys reading, writing and teaching her children 'rithmetic.

www.ingramcontent.com/pod-product-compliance
Lightning Source LLC
Chambersburg PA
CBHW050918120626
46552CB00004B/1640